W9-DEU-494

Country File
France

Celia Tidmarsh

A⁺

Smart Apple Media

First published in 2001 by Franklin Watts
96 Leonard Street, London EC2A 4XD, UK

Franklin Watts Australia
56 O'Riordan Street, Alexandria, NSW 2015

Country File: France produced for Franklin Watts by
Bender Richardson White, PO Box 266, Uxbridge, UK.

Project Editor: Lionel Bender, Text Editor: Peter
Harrison, Designer: Ben White, Picture Researcher:
Cathy Stastny, Media Conversion and Make-up:
Mike Pilley/Radius, Production: Kim Richardson
Graphics: Mike Pilley/Radius, Maps: Stefan Chabluk
Copyright © 2001 Bender Richardson White

For Franklin Watts, Series Editor: Adrian Cole, Art
Director: Jonathan Hair

Published in the United States by Smart Apple Media
1980 Lookout Drive, North Mankato, MN 56003

Library of Congress Cataloging-in-Publication Data

Tidmarsh, Celia.
France / by Celia Tidmarsh.
p. cm. — (Country files)
Includes index.
Summary: Describes the geography, economy,
government, people, transportation, education, and
culture of France.
ISBN 1-58340-202-0
1. France—Juvenile literature. [1. France.] I. Title.

DC17. T53 2002
944—dc21   2002017025

9 8 7 6 5 4 3 2 1

Picture Credits

Pages: 1: PhotoDisc Inc./Glen Allison. 3: Hutchison
Photo Library/Michael Macintyre. 4 top: PhotoDisc
Inc./Martial Colomb. 4 bottom: Hutchison Photo
Library/Robert Francis. 6: PhotoDisc Inc./Martial
Colomb. 8: DAS Photo/David Simson. 9: Eye Ubiquitous/
Paul Thompson. 10–11 top: PhotoDisc Inc./Martial
Colomb. 10 bottom: Lionheart Books. 12: Hutchison
Photo Library/J. C. Tordai. 13: Hutchison Photo Library.
15: Eye Ubiquitous/Julia Waterlow. 17 top: DAS Photo/
David Simson. 18 bottom: Hutchison Photo Library/
J. G. Fuller. 18 top: DAS Photo/David Simson.
18 bottom: Lionheart Books. 20: Hutchison Photo
Library/Michael Macintyre. 22: PhotoDisc Inc./Sami
Sarkis. 23: DAS Photo/David Simson. 24: PhotoDisc Inc./
Sami Sarkis. 25: Eye Ubiquitous/Mike Southern. 26:
Adam Woolfit/Corbis Images. 28: European Union
Audiovisual Department. 29: Reuters NewMedia
Inc./Corbis Images. 30: Lionheart Books. 31: DAS
Photo/David Simson.
Cover photo: Eye Ubiquitous/Paul Thompson.

Note

Most of the websites listed are in English. Some are in
French but have an option to view in English.

The Author

Celia Tidmarsh is a teacher trainer
specializing in geography. She has
written several books for children about
different countries of the world.

Contents

Welcome to France 4

The Land 6

The People 8

Urban and Rural Life 10

Farming and Fishing 13

Resources and Industry 14

Transportation 16

Education 19

Sports and Leisure 20

Daily Life and Religion 22

Arts and Media 24

Government 27

Place in the World 28

Database 30

Glossary 31

Index 32

Welcome to France

▲ The village of Huez in the Alps is snowbound in winter.

Fields and farmhouses near Rouen in northern France. ▼

France is the largest country in Europe. Its borders roughly follow the shape of a hexagon. At its northern edge is the English Channel and to the west is the Atlantic Ocean.

The Mediterranean Sea forms the southeast border, and the mountains of the Pyrénées are France's southwest limit. The Alps and Jura Mountains also make up most of the eastern border. It is only to the northeast that the border between France and neighboring countries is flat, low-lying land. The island of Corsica, roughly 112 miles (180 km) southeast of France, is also French territory.

Worldwide popularity and reputation

France has a variety of landscapes, including low-lying wetlands and high mountain ranges. There are many historic towns, such as Chartres, Orléans, and Reims, and chateaux (castles) such as those in the Loire valley, which attract tourists. The capital city is Paris, famous for the Louvre Museum and Notre Dame cathedral.

France is known worldwide for the food it produces, in particular its wine and cheese. The French have a reputation for being gourmets (a French word that means people who enjoy good food).

The Land

France has a varied landscape, with many different natural features. The climate is mainly temperate, but other conditions are found in, for example, the coastal and mountainous regions.

Across France there are rivers, lakes, salt marshes, and gentle hills, as well as mountains, flat plains, and coasts. Over half of France is low-lying, but there are also spectacular mountainous areas to the south and east. The highest peak in Europe, Mont Blanc, is in the French Alps.

Central France is characterized by an area of extinct volcanoes called the Massif Central.

Large rivers

France has four main rivers, the longest of which is the Loire. The river Seine flows through Paris, while in the south the river Garonne has cut deep gorges into the land. The Rhône, to the east, has formed a delta where it flows into the Mediterranean Sea.

Animals and Plants

Different areas of France are home to different types of animals and plants. For example:
- Chamois deer live in the Alps mountain range
- wild boar are found in forests in the north
- oak forests grow in the north and west
- in the south there are olive trees and herbs such as thyme and rosemary.

The mild climate and rich soil near Auxerre in Burgundy make the countryside good for growing grapes.

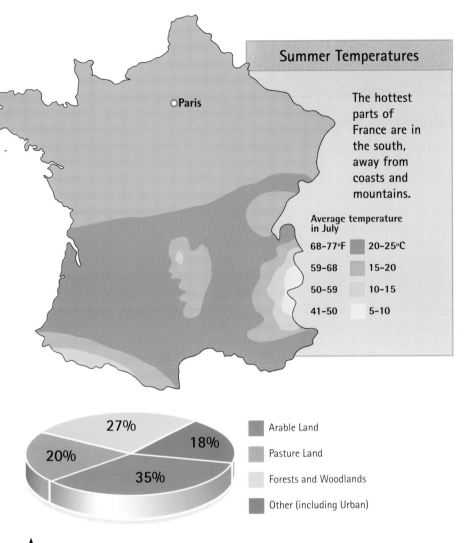

Summer Temperatures

The hottest parts of France are in the south, away from coasts and mountains.

Average temperature in July

68-77°F	20-25°C
59-68	15-20
50-59	10-15
41-50	5-10

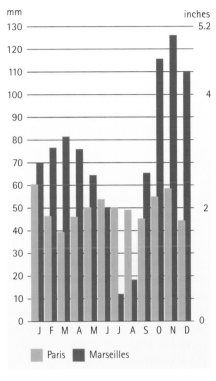

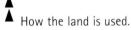

A comparison of the monthly rainfall of two major cities in France.

27%
20%
18%
35%

Arable Land
Pasture Land
Forests and Woodlands
Other (including Urban)

How the land is used.

Climate

Most of France has mild winters and warm summers. This is called a temperate climate. However, mountainous areas, such as the Alps, have much colder winters, which can bring heavy snowfalls.

The south, next to the Mediterranean Sea, has the hottest, driest summers and warmest winters in France. This is called a Mediterranean climate. Rain falls mainly in the autumn and winter.

Another feature of the climate in the south is the Mistral, a cold wind that blows down the Rhône valley at certain times of the year. It sometimes blows hard enough to damage whole fields of crops.

Web Search ▶▶

▶ www.abritel.fr/services/ abritel/uk/meteo24.html
Today's weather and forecast for France.

▶ www.meteo.fr
Weather and climate for France.

▶ www.franceguide.com
General information about France, including maps, travel, and tourist sites.

7

The People

With fewer babies being born and people living longer, France now has a very slow-growing, aging population. The people that make up the French nation have many different origins. A shared official language helps to build a sense of national identity.

The population of France is just under 59 million. At present it is growing at about 0.3 percent a year. This is because people are choosing to have small families with only one or two children. As a result the percentage of elderly people in France is increasing, while the percentage of population under 15 years is diminishing.

A population of mixed origins

Most modern French people are descended from the Celtic Gauls, who moved into what is now France from 1500 to 500 B.C., from the Romans, and from the Franks, a group of West Germanic people who took over the region from about A.D. 500. More recently there have also been immigrants from the Middle East, Portugal, Russia, Southeast Asia, and North Africa.

▲ Inside Galeries Lafayette department store in Paris. French people and tourists shop here for all kinds of goods.

Population since 1970. Overall, the population is getting older. In 1970, 67 percent of people were over age 20; in 2000, the figure was 74 percent. ▼

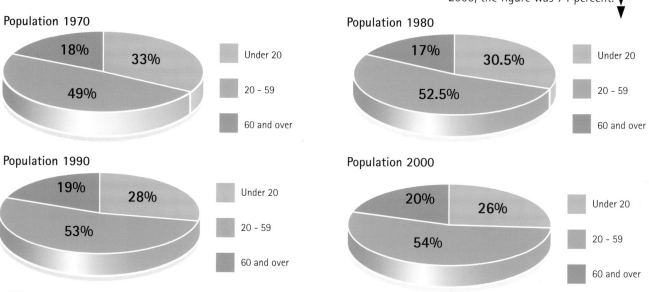

Population 1970
- 18%
- 33%
- 49%
- Under 20
- 20 - 59
- 60 and over

Population 1980
- 17%
- 30.5%
- 52.5%
- Under 20
- 20 - 59
- 60 and over

Population 1990
- 19%
- 28%
- 53%
- Under 20
- 20 - 59
- 60 and over

Population 2000
- 20%
- 26%
- 54%
- Under 20
- 20 - 59
- 60 and over

A common language

French is the official national language. It mainly grew out of Latin, the language of the Romans. Some areas in France have kept traditional languages—Flemish in the far north, Breton in Brittany, Basque and Catalan in the areas bordering Spain, and Provençal in Provence.

French is also the official language in Belgium, Switzerland, Luxembourg, Canada, and more than 30 countries in Africa, the Caribbean, and the Pacific islands that formed part of the French colonial empire. Altogether, about 200 million people in the world speak French.

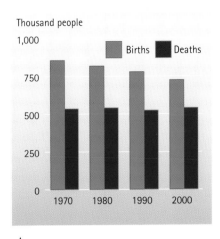

Thousand people

▲ Changes in numbers of births and deaths in France since 1970.

◄◄ Artists from all over the world sit and paint in the Montmartre district of Paris. Situated in the shadow of Sacre-Coeur, one of the city's oldest churches, the area is filled with traditional French restaurants.

Web Search ►►

► www.paris.org
A guide to Paris, the capital city.

► www.britannica.com
The Encyclopedia Britannica entry on France.

► www.brittany-bretagne.com
Guide to the northwest of France, the Breton region.

► www.odci.gov/cia/publications/factbook/geos/fr.html
The US Central Intelligence Agency factbook on France, including maps.

Urban and Rural Life

The population of France is spread very unevenly throughout the country. Over the past 50 years more people have moved to urban areas. This is largely because of the higher number of job opportunities available when compared to rural areas.

Mountainous regions, such as the Pyrénées, have less than 40 people per square mile (15 per sq km). People choose to live in low-lying parts of the country, such as the area around Paris, because it is easier to farm and build on the land. The Paris area has more than 385 people per square mile (150 per sq km).

There has been a big shift in population from the countryside to cities since World War II. By 2000 France had 44.5 million people living in towns and cities. The largest cities include Paris, Marseilles, and Lyons.

Many villages in France, like this one in Normandy, lie among hills and are surrounded by farmland and trees. ▼

People on the move

Urban areas offer more job opportunities in offices, shops, and banks. People are also moving to some areas because they have a pleasant climate, such as the area along the Mediterranean coast.

People in urban areas have traditionally lived in apartments in large old buildings around town or city centers. After World War II there was a housing shortage, so modern, high-rise apartment buildings were built on the edges of large urban areas. Those people that could afford to began to move to detached houses in the suburbs.

Renting farmhouses, building new homes

In isolated rural areas, farmhouses have been left empty as people have moved into towns and cities. In parts of Brittany and the Massif Central some farmers have rented out these farmhouses to tourists and used the money to build new houses for themselves.

▲ A view over Paris, the largest and most populated city in France. To the right of center stands the Eiffel Tower.

% of Total Population

▲ How the urban population has changed since 1950.

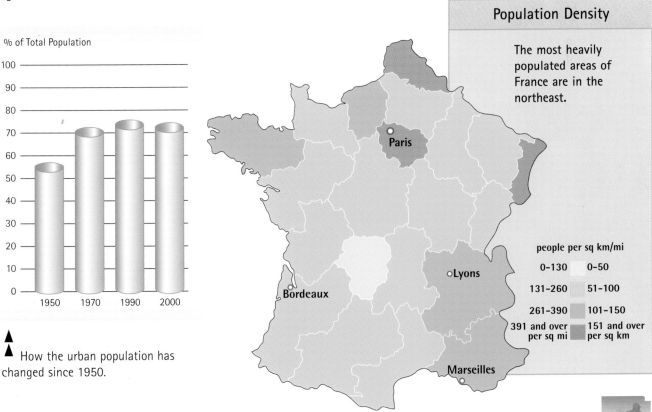

Population Density

The most heavily populated areas of France are in the northeast.

people per sq km/mi

0–130	0–50
131–260	51–100
261–390	101–150
391 and over per sq mi	151 and over per sq km

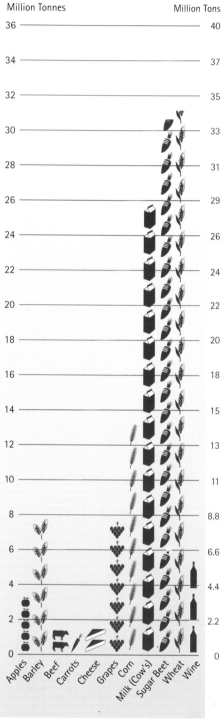

Million Tonnes   Million Tons

36 — 40
34 — 37
32 — 35
30 — 33
28 — 31
26 — 29
24 — 26
22 — 24
20 — 22
18 — 20
16 — 18
14 — 15
12 — 13
10 — 11
8 — 8.8
6 — 6.6
4 — 4.4
2 — 2.2
0 — 0

Apples   Barley   Beef   Carrots   Cheese   Grapes   Corn   Milk (Cow's)   Sugar Beet   Wheat   Wine

▲ A fisherman returns to harbor with his catch of crabs.

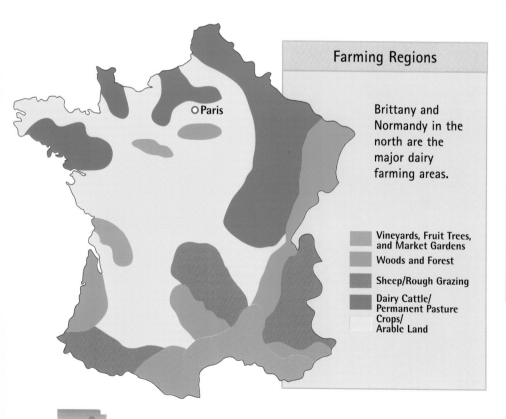

Farming Regions

Brittany and Normandy in the north are the major dairy farming areas.

- Vineyards, Fruit Trees, and Market Gardens
- Woods and Forest
- Sheep/Rough Grazing
- Dairy Cattle/ Permanent Pasture
- Crops/ Arable Land

○ Paris

▲ Main farming products. France ranks in the world's top 10 producers of meat, milk, and various fruits and vegetables.

Farming and Fishing

Fishing is an important economic activity in the coastal regions of France. As well as the main ports such as Cherbourg, and Quîmper, there are small fishing boats operating from most coastal villages.

Fishing boats from France work around the coasts of Europe and Iceland, the east coast of Canada, and the west coast of Africa.

The French eat about 66 pounds (30 kg) of fish a year per person, compared to 15 pounds (7 kg) in the United States.

Even though farming and fishing provide the French population with most of what they need to eat, these industries do not employ many people. Nevertheless, farmers contribute to the French economy by producing goods for the export market.

Over half of the land in France is used for farming. Wheat and corn are grown where land is low-lying and the climate is cooler and wetter. Cattle, reared for milk and beef, are found in many regions, apart from around the Mediterranean where it is too hot for them. Sheep are found mainly in the mountainous areas. Grape vines and fruit, such as peaches and lemons, are grown mainly in the warmer, more southern areas.

Changes in farming

In the past, farming was especially important to France because the economy was based on agriculture. Today, only four percent of the work force are farmers.

However, because France is able to grow more food than it needs and can sell the surplus to other countries, farming is still an important industry for the nation.

France is the second largest food exporter in the world. In the 1940s, one farmer could grow enough food to feed five people. By 2000, one farmer could feed more than 30 people. This is because many farms have become bigger and use more machinery, fertilizers, and pesticides. In the more remote rural areas, farms are still small and farming methods are more traditional.

◄◄ Farmers pick grapes from a vineyard near Cahors, in southwest France.

Resources and Industry

The natural resources of France were once used to provide energy and raw materials for French manufacturing industries. Nowadays it is cheaper to import such resources. Many manufacturing industries no longer employ as many people as in the past; service industries now provide most jobs.

Until the 1960s, most of the energy used came from coal mined in northern France. When this began to run out, oil and gas were used, although most of this had to be imported. Today, electricity is mainly supplied by nuclear power stations; they produce over 80 percent of France's energy needs. Hydroelectric power is also produced, using the fast-flowing rivers of mountainous areas such as the Alps. There is also a tidal power station at Rance in Normandy, and wind power stations exist in Britanny.

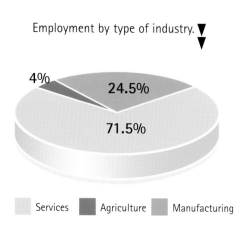

Employment by type of industry. ▼

- 4%
- 24.5%
- 71.5%

Services   Agriculture   Manufacturing

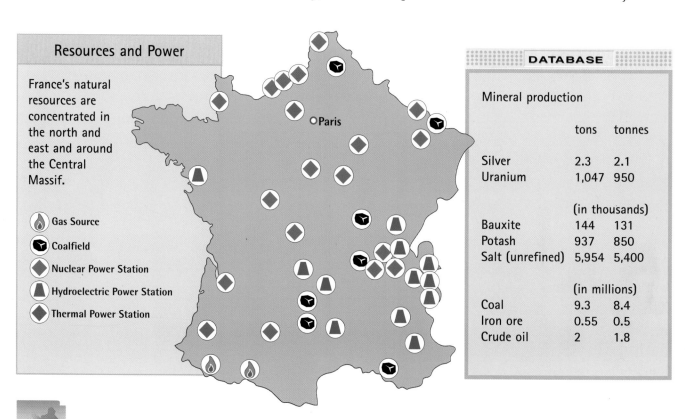

Resources and Power

France's natural resources are concentrated in the north and east and around the Central Massif.

- ⬙ Gas Source
- ⬤ Coalfield
- ◆ Nuclear Power Station
- ⬠ Hydroelectric Power Station
- ⬟ Thermal Power Station

○ Paris

DATABASE

Mineral production

	tons	tonnes
Silver	2.3	2.1
Uranium	1,047	950
	(in thousands)	
Bauxite	144	131
Potash	937	850
Salt (unrefined)	5,954	5,400
	(in millions)	
Coal	9.3	8.4
Iron ore	0.55	0.5
Crude oil	2	1.8

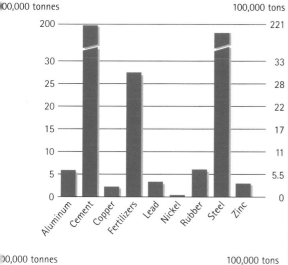

◄◄ Quantities of materials and manufactured goods produced by French industry.

Manufacturing and mining

Smelting and shipbuilding are still major industries. Minerals mined on a small scale in northwest France include bauxite (used to produce aluminum), potash, and sodium chloride (salt).

The car and electronics industries are also important for France's economy. Companies such as Citroën, Renault, and the electronics corporation Thomson Multimedia sell their products internationally. The French aircraft and aerospace industries are also respected worldwide.

Service industries

The new growth areas in French industry are finance and insurance, advertising, telecommunications, the hotel trade, and information technology. France is also a world leader in biotechnology, robotics, and medicine.

▲ A tanker fills up at an oil refinery at Le Havre in northern France.

Web Search ►►

► **www.cenerg.cma.fr**
Information from France's Center for Energy Studies.

► **www.minefi.gouv.fr**
Website of the Ministry of Economy, Finance, and Industry.

► **www.cea.fr**
Information from France's atomic energy authority.

Transportation

Getting Around in Paris

THE METRO: this is the underground rail network. No point in Paris is more than 550 yards (500 m) from an underground station.

BUSES: there is an extensive network of bus routes, but the heavy traffic in Paris can mean slow journeys.

TAXIS: these can be flagged down anywhere or found at taxi stands.

RIVER TAXIS (boats): during the summer a shuttle service stops at the main tourist sites on or near the river Seine in Paris.

All the road, rail, and air networks in France carry a large number of passengers and great quantities of freight. There are also strong transportation links with other countries by road, rail, air, and sea.

France has a large highway (autoroute) network. On some autoroutes drivers have to pay money—called "tolls"—to use them. There is also a network of main roads and smaller roads. Road transportation is used widely to carry both passengers and freight.

The rail network is made up of main lines radiating out from Paris. These include special tracks for the high-speed train system called the Train à Grande Vitesse (TGV). Traveling by TGV is often even faster than going by air. Air travel is important within France because of the size of the country. Airports furthest away from Paris are particularly busy because of this. For example, Nice handles more than six million passengers a year.

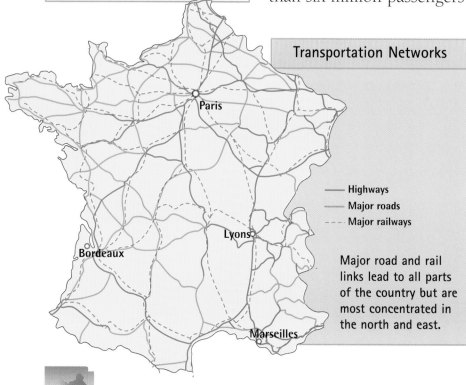

Transportation Networks

— Highways
— Major roads
--- Major railways

Major road and rail links lead to all parts of the country but are most concentrated in the north and east.

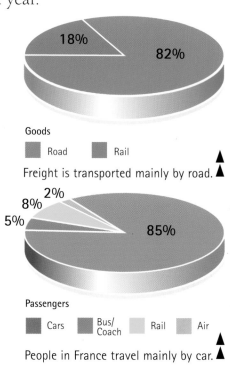

Goods
■ Road ■ Rail

Freight is transported mainly by road. ▲

Passengers
■ Cars ■ Bus/Coach ■ Rail ■ Air

People in France travel mainly by car. ▲

▲
▲ The Eurostar train takes passengers from London to Paris through the Channel Tunnel. A TGV train tunnel is now being built through the Pyrénées to link southern France and Spain.

◄◄ Travelers emerge from the Métro, the underground railway of Paris.

🌐 **Web Search ►►**

► www.smartweb.fr/aero/
index.html
Details of Paris airports and flights

►www.smartweb.fr/guide.
transport/index.html
Information about transportation in Paris (includes map).

Links with other countries

France's road and rail networks are linked to the rest of Europe. The Mont Blanc road tunnel links France and Italy. The Channel Tunnel links France and England. There are international airports in many of the larger towns. Sea ferry services run from French ports to England, Ireland, Spain, North Africa, and Sardinia.

▲ Every school in France and in the overseas French colonies has a similar curriculum. Children increasingly use computers in school.

▶▶ Many small villages in France have a local school where children of very different ages attend classes together and are taught several subjects by the same teacher.

Education

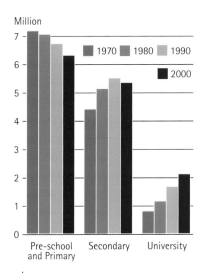

Million

7 —
6 —
5 —
4 —
3 —
2 —
1 —
0 —

1970 1980 1990

2000

Pre-school   Secondary   University
and Primary

Numbers of pupils in each category of education.

In France, education can be public or private. Most children go to public schools that are run by the Ministry of National Education.

Education is free for all children between 6 and 16. It is also compulsory, meaning that all children of these ages must go to school. Some children go to nursery schools when they are two years old. Children attend primary schools between the ages of 6 and 11. After primary school they go to the local secondary school until they are 15 or 16, when they choose whether they want to continue studying or leave school and train for a job.

The baccalaureat

Students study a wide range of subjects. When they are 16, they can choose to concentrate on languages, economics, or science, but they also continue with the other subjects. When they are 18, students can take the university entrance exam, called the general baccalaureat. If they pass, they can go to one of the 77 universities in France.

Students who leave school at 16 can go to a technical college to learn a skill that will help them get a job. In all schools, children do not have to wear school uniforms.

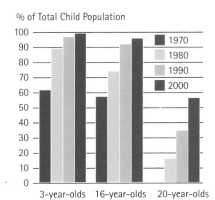

% of Total Child Population

100
90
80
70
60
50
40
30
20
10
0

1970
1980
1990
2000

3-year-olds   16-year-olds   20-year-olds

Percentage of selected age groups who enrolled in education.

Class time and Vacations

The school day lasts from 8:30 a.m. to 4:30 p.m., with two hours for lunch. Most primary and some secondary school children in France go to school on Saturday mornings. There are no lessons on Wednesday afternoons. This time is used for sports.

Summer vacation lasts nine weeks, which is longer than most other European countries but shorter than the American 12-week vacation.

Web Search ▶▶

▶ www.education.fr
Details of education in France.

▶ www.edutel.fr
Site of the French Ministry of Education.

Sports and Leisure

Nowadays, more than ever before, French people have money and time to pursue leisure interests. About 70 percent of families take a vacation at least once a year. Most of these vacations are taken in France. Watching and playing sports is also very popular.

The French enjoy watching sports such as soccer, rugby, basketball, tennis, car racing, skiing, and bicycling. Soccer has become even more popular since the national team won the World Cup and the European Cup. A number of famous sporting events take place every year, such as the French Open Tennis Championship and the Tour de France bicycle race.

THE TOUR DE FRANCE

This is the most famous bicycle race in the world. Over 200 cyclists take part every year. The race takes three weeks and is approximately 2,500 miles (4,000 km) long.

The route changes each year. Ordinary roads are used and closed to traffic. Thousands of people go to watch and cheer on their favourite cyclists.

Some parts of the race go through high, steep mountain passes in the Pyrénées and the Alps. The finish line is always on the Champs Elysées, the famous avenue in Paris.

▶▶ The Tour de France race leaders. The cyclists are followed by race supervisors, police, and television camera crews on motorcycles.

Outdoor activities

Water sports such as swimming and diving are very popular both in the sea and on inland lakes such as Lac d'Annecy in the Alps. Mountains such as the Alps and the Pyrénées offer the chance to ski and snowboard in the winter and to hike in the summer.

French people enjoy taking long vacations in the summer. Many families stay at seaside resorts or in gîtes (rented vacation homes) in the countryside in France. Tourism has become a very important industry, providing many jobs and valuable income for local rural economies. About 60 million tourists come to France every year from abroad and visit its hotels, restaurants, and tourist attractions such as EuroDisney near Paris. Since 1980 the amount of money tourists spend in France has increased dramatically.

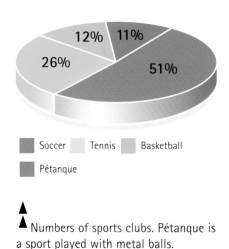

■ Soccer ■ Tennis ■ Basketball
■ Pétanque

▲ Numbers of sports clubs. Pétanque is a sport played with metal balls.

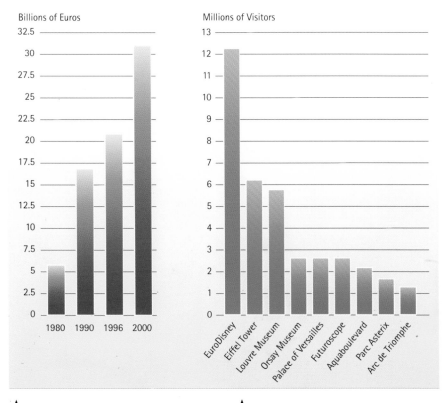

▲ Growth in money spent by tourists in France, in billions of euros.

▲ Yearly visitors at the most popular tourist sites in France.

Web Search ►►

► www.smartweb.fr/ people/cup98
Pictures of the 1998 World Cup.

► www.smartweb.fr/ people/tourdefrance
Pictures of the Tour de France.

► www.tourisme.fr
French Tourist Office website.

► www.france.com/ francescape
General tourist information.

► www.paris.org
Tourist information about Paris.

Daily Life and Religion

French people come from a variety of religious and cultural backgrounds. They spend almost eight percent of their income on eating out in restaurants.

The French work an average of 39 hours a week. Daily working hours are from about 8 a.m. until 6 p.m., often with a two-hour lunch break. Most offices, construction sites, and factories are closed on weekends.

Shops

French people buy goods at a range of retail outlets. There are small shops selling particular kinds of food, such as charcuteries that sell cooked meats and boulangeries that sell bread. There are also hypermarchés (enormous supermarkets) selling all types of food and drink, as well as clothes and household equipment. The small shops are found in villages and in town centers; hypermarchés are usually built on the outskirts of town. Most towns also have a weekly street market.

% of Households Owning

Ownership of electronic goods.

Armed forces

France's armed forces total 380,820 troops, divided into land, air, and sea forces. There is also a police force, called the gendarmerie, which is part of the armed forces. At the age of 18 all French males have to spend 10 months in one of these forces. This is called compulsory military service. However, from 2002 on the French armed forces will consist entirely of volunteers.

Notre Dame in Paris, one of the most famous churches in France. ▼

◄◄ Fruit for sale at a street market in France.

Web Search ►►

► www.sante.gouv.fr
General health information.

► www.defense.gouv.fr
Website of the Ministry of Defense.

► www.info-europe.fr
The European Union website for all aspects of French life.

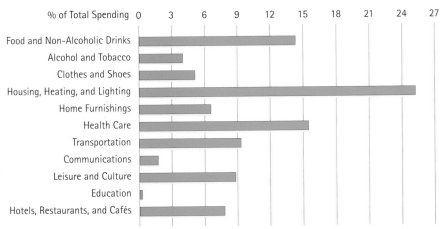

% of Total Spending	
Food and Non-Alcoholic Drinks	
Alcohol and Tobacco	
Clothes and Shoes	
Housing, Heating, and Lighting	
Home Furnishings	
Health Care	
Transportation	
Communications	
Leisure and Culture	
Education	
Hotels, Restaurants, and Cafés	

◄◄ How French households spend their money. The cost of living in France is high compared to many non-European countries, but in Europe it is not much above average.

Religion

There is no official state religion in France. About 88 percent of the French population say they are Roman Catholic. The second largest religious group follow the Islamic faith: there are over three million Muslims in France, many of them immigrants or children of immigrants from North Africa. There are also about one million Protestants and about 500,000 Jews.

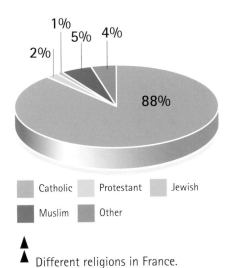

1% 5% 4%
2%
88%

Catholic   Protestant   Jewish
Muslim   Other

▲ Different religions in France.

Arts and Media

Famous French people in art, literature, music, and movies

Claude Monet	Artist
Auguste Renoir	Artist
Voltaire	Writer
Marcel Proust	Writer
Georges Bizet	Composer
Claude Debussy	Composer
Edith Piaf	Popular singer
Sasha Distel	Popular singer
Jean Renoir	Film director
François Truffaut	Film director

People are attracted to the chateaux, cathedrals, and palaces in France. This is Palais Longchamp in Marseilles. ▼

France possesses some of the world's most famous museums and art galleries. It is also renowned for its cultural events, including the annual film festival in Cannes in southern France.

Some of the best known art galleries are found in Paris, including the Louvre and the Pompidou Center of Art and Culture. Over the years, many French artists have become known throughout the world, including the Impressionist painters Claude Monet and Auguste Renoir. France has produced several of the world's greatest writers, philosophers, singers, and composers of classical music.

Going to see films has been a popular leisure activity in France ever since the opening of the world's first public movie theater in Paris, in 1895. Even today, movie audiences are higher than in other European countries. In 1987, a unique theme park about movies, video, and visual technology, called Futuroscope, was opened near Poitiers.

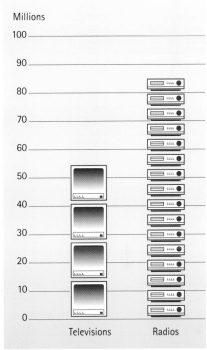

◄◄ These unusual structures form part of the fountain outside the Pompidou Center in Paris.

Millions

▲
▲ Ownership of televisions and radios.

The national press

Daily newspapers are published in about 40 French cities, and more than 12 in Paris itself. Two of the daily national papers, Le Monde and Le Figaro, are world famous. There are also daily regional papers, for example Ouest-France, which sells more copies in France every day than any other paper. As well as newspapers, there are magazines such as Paris-Match and Elle.

Television and radio

With 116 channels, including cable and pay-TV, French TV viewers have plenty to choose from. The average time spent watching television is 16 hours per week. There are hundreds of radio broadcast stations. Most are local commercial stations that broadcast not only in French but in English and other European languages.

Web Search ►►

► **www.lemonde.fr**
Read the French newspaper Le Monde.

► **www.cplus.fr**
Television viewing details from Canal+ broadcast station.

► **www.paris.org/Musees**
Details of museums in Paris.

► **www.futuroscope.fr**
Website of Futuroscope theme park.

► **www.louvre.fr**
View the collection of the Louvre museum in Paris.

▲ The Government office building in the town of Nancy in northeast France. The office deals with law and order for local and overseas départements.

French overseas départements. ▼

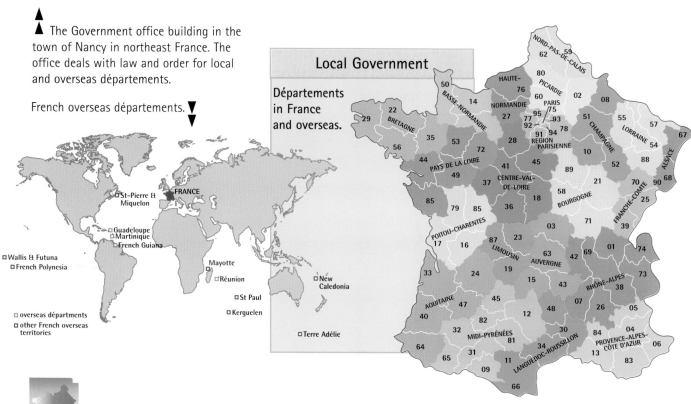

Local Government

Départements in France and overseas.

□ overseas départements
□ other French overseas territories

St-Pierre & Miquelon

FRANCE

□ Guadeloupe
□ Martinique
□ French Guiana

□ Wallis & Futuna
□ French Polynesia

Mayotte

□ Réunion

□ St Paul

□ Kerguelen

□ New Caledonia

□ Terre Adélie

NORD-PAS-DE-CALAIS
62
59
80
HAUTE-
76
PICARDIE
02
08
50
BASSE-NORMANDIE
14
NORMANDIE
60
75 PARIS
51
55
57
22
27
77
95
93
CHAMPAGNE
LORRAINE
54
67
29
BRETAGNE
92
78
88
35
53
28
91 94
10
52
ALSACE
68
56
72
REGION PARISIENNE
45
89
70
90
44
PAYS DE LA LOIRE
41
21
58
FRANCHE-COMTÉ
25
49
37
CENTRE-VAL-DE-LOIRE
18
BOURGOGNE
85
79
85
36
03
71
39
POITOU-CHARENTES
87
23
01
74
17
16
LIMOUSIN
63
69
33
24
19
AUVERGNE
42
73
15
43
RHONE-ALPES
38
AQUITAINE
45
07
26
05
47
12
48
40
82
30
04
32
MIDI-PYRÉNÉES
81
34
84
PROVENCE-ALPES-CÔTE D'AZUR
06
64
31
11
LANGUEDOC-ROUSSILLON
13
83
65
09
66

Government

France is a democracy in which the people elect members of the National Assembly and Senate, which together make up parliament.

France does not have a royal family; it became a republic in 1789. The president is the head of state and appoints the prime minister. The president is elected for seven years.

The National Assembly has 577 deputies elected by the people for five years. The Senate has 321 senators elected for nine years by local officials and the National Assembly. The president has the power to make the major decisions but needs support from the prime minister and parliament. If the president and prime minister are from different political parties, this can lead to conflict.

Political parties

The main political parties are the Socialist Party, the Communist Party, the Republican Party, and the Democratic Union. There are also regional and local governments. France is divided into 22 regions. Each region is divided into areas called départements. There are 96 of these in mainland France and five overseas. Each département has a council elected by the residents. These councils have the power to make local decisions.

Overseas départements

Départements such as Guadaloupe in the West Indies have the same rights as those in France. Each has a regional council that makes local decisions and elects members to the French parliament based in Paris. They are subject to French laws and have French schools, police, and currency. From 2002 the new national currency is the euro, which replaces the French franc.

Département Names and Numbers

Most départements are named after geographical features, mainly rivers, such as Dorgogne in the region of Aquitaine and Tarn in the Midi-Pyrénées.

Every département has a number. These are used on car registration plates. For example, number 75 is for the center of Paris.

Web Search ▶▶

▶ www.dir.yahoo.com/ Regional/Countries/ France/Departments
Information on each département.

▶ www.premier-ministre. gouv.fr
Website of France's Prime Minister.

▶ www.assemblee-nat.fr
Information about the National Assembly.

▶ www.tahitiweb.com
Private website of the island of Tahiti in French Polynesia.

Place in the World

Chronology of Historical Events

1500–500 B.C.
The Gauls move into France.

52 B.C. to A.D. 500
France is overrun by the Romans.

768–814
Charlemagne, king of the Franks, rules and takes over more territory for France.

1337–1453
Battles between France and England, including the Battle of Agincourt (1415).

1562–98
The Wars of Religion between the Catholics and Protestants in France.

1643–1715
Louis XIV is king.

1789
The French Revolution begins.

1792
The king is overthrown and France is made a republic.

1799–1804
Napoleon Bonaparte takes over as ruler and later becomes Emperor of France.

1804–12
The French army, led by Napoleon Bonaparte, wins a number of battles and occupies much of Europe.

1815
Napoleon and his army are defeated by a combined English/Prussian/Dutch force at the Battle of Waterloo.

1870–71
France is defeated in battle by the Prussians in the Franco-Prussian War.

1914–18
At war with Germany in World War I.

1939–45
At war with Germany in World War II.

France has played an important part in European history for over 1,500 years. Its role in the wider world began with the founding of colonies in North America in 1731 and continues into the 21st century.

France is a key member of the European Union (EU). In fact, the idea for the EU first came from France after World War II. The aim was to build friendship between France and Germany in order to prevent any more wars between the two countries.

As the EU has grown to include many members, France has continued to play a central role in it. France has the second largest economy in the EU and therefore contributes large sums of money to paying for the costs of building the union. Most French people like being members of the EU and support its policies and plans.

The present political system in France was set up in 1958 when Charles de Gaulle became president. Soon after, France was involved in fighting with Vietnam and Algeria, two of its colonies that wanted independence. By 1969 all its colonies had become independent countries. Today, France still has strong links with these countries.

May 9, 1950—at a meeting in Paris of foreign leaders, the French foreign minister reads out the terms for cooperation between European nations. This has become today's European Union. ▼

◄◄ At Kourou in French Guiana a nose cone containing satellites for European television companies is being taken to a launch pad to be loaded onto a rocket and carried into space. France plays a major role in the European Space Agency, and its rocket site in French Guiana is used by many countries.

Web Search ►►

► www.franceway.com
French history.

► www.france.net.au
Australian-based website for the French embassy.

► www.gouv.qc.ca
Information on Quebec in Canada.

► www.diplomatie.gouv.fr
Website for the French Ministry of Foreign Affairs.

► www.legifrance.gouv.fr
General information on the French constitution.

► www.finances.gouv.fr/euro
Website of the Ministry of Finance of the French Government.

► www.europa.eu.int/index_en.htm
General information on the EU.

% of Total

- Food/Live Animals
- Drinks/Tobacco
- Raw Materials (Ores etc.)
- Fuels/Energy
- Chemicals
- Manufactured Goods
- Machinery/Transport Equipment
- Other Goods and Services

Exports   Imports

◄◄ Comparative figures for France's imports and exports. Its major trading partners are other members of the EU.

29

Area:
211,207 sq mi (547,026 sq km)

Population size:
58,519,000

Capital city:
Paris (population 2,152,423)

Other major cities:
Marseilles, Lyons, Toulouse

Longest river:
Loire 3,320 ft (1,012 km)

Highest mountain:
Mont Blanc 15,771 ft (4,807 m)

Largest lake:
Lac Léman 92 sq mi (239 sq km)

Flag:
Red, white, and blue vertical
stripes, known as the tricolor.
Dates from the French Revolution
in 1789. Blue and red were the
city colors of Paris, where the
revolution began. White was the
old French royal color.

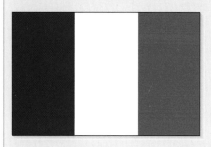

Official language:
French.

Currency:
From 2002 euros; before that
French francs.

Major resources:
Uranium, potash, salt, oil, iron ore

Major exports:
Machinery/transportation
equipment (for example, cars, tires,
aircraft); manufactured goods (for
example, TVs, radios, computers)

National holidays:
New Year's Day (January 1)
Easter (late March/early April)
May Day (May 1)
WWII Victory Day (May 8)
Ascension Day: 40th day after
  Easter (May)

Pentecost: seventh Sunday after
  Easter (mid-May/mid-June)
Whit Monday (mid-May/mid-June)
Bastille Day (July 14)
Assumption Day (August 15)
All Saints' Day (November 1)
Remembrance Day (November 11)
Christmas (December 25)

Religions:
Roman Catholicism, Islam,
Protestantism, Judaism

Glossary

AGING POPULATION
A population in which the proportion of people over 60 years of age is increasing, and the proportion of those under 15 is decreasing.

BACCALAUREAT
The exam taken by French students at the age of 18 to qualify for a place at a university.

BASQUES
People who originate from and live in the southwest area of France and the northwest area of Spain around the Bay of Biscay.

BRETONS
People who originate from and live in the region of Brittany.

CLIMATE
The average weather conditions experienced in one area over a period of time.

COLONIES
Countries which were taken over and ruled by other countries.

DELTA
Name given to new land which is built up out of sand and silt deposited by a river as it flows into the sea.

EUROPEAN UNION (EU)
A grouping of European countries that all trade with each other on commonly agreed terms.

EXPORTS
Goods and services sold by one country to others.

EXTINCT VOLCANO
A volcano that will never erupt again.

EURO
The currency that the countries of the European Union have agreed they will use in order to trade with each other.

FREIGHT
Goods and products that are carried by trucks, trains, and ships.

GORGE
A steep-sided, deep valley cut into rock by a river.

HIGH-TECHNOLOGY INDUSTRIES
Industries and businesses that make or use the latest technology.

IMMIGRANTS
People who move from one country to live in another.

IMPORTS
Goods and services bought by one country from others.

IMPRESSIONIST
Describes a group of French artists who achieved fame in France and abroad between the 1860s and 1880s.

MANUFACTURING INDUSTRIES
Industries that make products from raw materials.

NATURAL VEGETATION
Plants and trees that grow in an area when humans have not interfered.

POPULATION DENSITY
The number of people living in an area such as one square mile or kilometer.

RAW MATERIALS
The original materials needed to make products; for example, iron ore is needed to make steel.

RESOURCES
Things that can be used; for example, coal can be used to make electricity.

RURAL
In the country.

SERVICE INDUSTRIES
Industries which provide a service to people rather than make products.

SUBURBS
Areas of housing between a town or city center and the countryside.

TEMPERATE CLIMATE
A climate that has mild winters and warm summers.

TRAIN DE GRANDE VITESSE (TGV)
High-speed train developed in 1981 that travels at up to 190 mph (300 kph).

URBAN
In towns and cities.

Index

air travel 16, 17
Alps Mountains 4, 6, 7, 14, 20, 21
animals 6
armed forces 22
arts 24, 25

Brittany 9, 11, 12, 14
Burgundy 6

Channel Tunnel 17
Chartres 4
cities 11, 30
climate 6, 7, 11
coasts 6, 7, 11, 12, 13
Corsica 4
currency 27, 30

départements 26, 27

education 18, 19, 23
Eiffel Tower 11
electricity 14, 15
employment 13, 14, 21, 22
energy 14
euro 27, 30
European Union 28, 29
exports 13, 15, 29, 30

farming 12, 13
fishing 12, 13
flag 30
food 4, 12, 13, 23

Garonne, river 6

Gauls 8, 28
government 26, 27

history 28
holidays 30
hydroelectricity 14

imports 29
industry 14, 15

Jura Mountains 4

landscape 4, 6
languages 8, 9, 19, 25, 30
Le Havre 15
Loire, river 6, 30
Louvre 4, 24
Lyons 10, 30

manufacturing 14, 15
Marseilles 10, 24, 30
Massif Central 6, 11, 14
media 24, 25
Mediterranean 4, 6, 7, 11, 13
mining 15
Mistral 7
Mont Blanc 6, 17, 30
movies 24, 25

newspapers 25
Notre Dame 4, 22

Paris 4, 6, 8, 9, 10, 16, 21, 22, 24, 25, 26, 27, 28, 30
parliament 27

Poitiers 21, 24
politics 27
population 8, 9, 10, 11, 13, 30
Pyrénées Mountains 4, 10, 17, 20, 21

Quebec 9
Quimper 13

radio 25
railways 16, 17
rainfall 7
religion 23, 30
resources 14, 30
Rhône, river 6, 7
roads 16, 17, 20
Rouen 4
rural 11, 21

schools 18, 19, 27
Seine, river 6, 16
shopping 8, 22, 23
sports 20, 21
Strasbourg 7

television 24, 25, 29
Tour de France 20
tourism 11, 21
trains 16, 17
transportation 16, 17

universities 19
urban 10

volcanoes, extinct 6